WALT DISNEY'S Donald Duck and CHIP 'N' DALE

Pictures by the WALT DISNEY STUDIO

Adapted by

STAN WALSH and GENE WOLFE

A WHITMAN BOOK

Western Publishing Company, Inc.

Racine, Wisconsin

"Donald Duck!"

The sharp, scolding voice woke Donald from a lovely dream. Blinking, he sat up in the hammock and looked at his neighbors who were standing in a circle around him.

"Wh-what's going on here?" he demanded. "Is something wrong?"

"There certainly is," said the lady who lived next door. "Donald, this is Clean-up Week, and we've all been busy for days painting our houses. Now, we want to know when you plan to fix up *your* house. It's the worst-looking place on the block."

"Oh, it's not so bad," Donald said, looking at the chipped and peeling paint. "I'll tend to it some day."

"You'll paint it *today*," snapped the lady, "or you'll have all of us to deal with." And away they went, muttering and shaking their heads.

there were purple scallops around
every window—

a big, funny face decorated the front
door—
every shutter had a different pattern
painted on it—

and the roof was covered with pink
and yellow polka dots.

If you had happened to pass Donald Duck's house that evening you would have seen a strange sight. All the neighbors were gathered in a circle beside the house. They looked very angry.

In the center of the circle stood Donald Duck. He had a paint brush in his hand and a bucket of paint.

"And what's more," the lady next door was saying, "we're going to stay right here until you've cleaned up every bit of this mess, Donald. Now get busy!"

"That's right, get busy," echoed two little voices. And if you had happened to look up at that very moment, you would have seen two little chipmunks chuckling to themselves high in the maple tree.